This book is dedicated to John, my incredible husband and rock, and to Lexi, Johnny and Robbie, the world's original Spriitelees.
M.C.S.

To my wonderful husband, Gordy, whose unyielding love has been such a source of comfort. And to our beautiful son, Christopher, who has brought immeasurable happiness into our lives.
M.A.S.

Thank you Elsa and Frank Stankard for three invaluable gifts— kindness, love, and faith.

☙ ☙ ☙

Cover and book design by Arrow Graphics, Inc.
info@arrow1.com
Printed in China

First Edition 2006

Publisher's Cataloging-in-Publication
(Provided by Quality Books, Inc.)

Stankard, Marcia C.
The Spriitelees : a Christmas tale about kindness / written by Marcia C.
Stankard ; illustrated by Melinda A. Shoals. -- 1st ed.
p. cm.
SUMMARY: It's Christmas Eve and Santa's elves have the flu.
Spriitelees kindly volunteer to help. One Spriitelee's generous
deed earns him a special reward. Audience: Ages 3-7.

LCCN 2005908706
ISBN-13: 978-0-9773460-0-4
ISBN-10: 0-9773460-0-5

1. Generosity--Juvenile fiction.
2. Kindness--Juvenile fiction. 3. Christmas--Juvenile fiction.
4. Santa Claus--Juvenile fiction. [1. Generosity--Fiction.
2. Kindness--Fiction. 3. Christmas--Fiction.
4. Santa Claus--Fiction. 5. Stories in rhyme.]
I. Shoals, Melinda A., ill. II. Title.

PZ8.3.S787Spr 2006   [E]
QBI05-600187

The Spriitelees

Written by Marcia C. Stankard

Illustrated by Melinda A. Shoals

Dear Cate,
Keep brightening the
world with kindness!
Marcia Stankard
Holidays 2006

SPRiiTELEE ENTERPRISES

WESTWOOD, MASSACHUSETTS
www.Spriitelee.com

One Christmas Eve harsh winter winds blew
and Santa's elves came down with the flu.
Santa panicked. "What will I do?
My reindeer aren't ready, the presents aren't wrapped,
my list isn't written, and I need a nap!"

"I'd help," sighed Mrs. Claus warming chicken soup with noodles,
"but I'm handing out tissues by the oodles and oodles!
Christmas may not happen, I am sorry to say.
There's too much to do in only one day!"

Santa needed help. That was clear.
But who would step in? No one lived near.
The North Pole is as high
as a twinkling star.
If help were to come, it must come from afar.

Luckily to the south, far below the North Pole,
there exists a small island, Kindness Grove Knoll.
Home to small children with gleeful, kind hearts
Spriitelees looking for places to spread kindness sparks.

Sparking and zooming are skills that they learn
and a sparkpack is something they each have to earn.
By acting kindly three times in a row,
they create the magic that makes sparkpacks grow.

That Christmas Eve seven Spriitelees craving fun
zoomed off their island.
Well...all zoomed but one!

The grounded Spriitelee, Bob,
still in spark school,
had to help one more person.
That was the rule.
"Please take me with you!
Look! No homework today!"
Bob called to his friends,
eager to play.

Passing the North Pole, pulling Bob along,
the group quickly learned that something was wrong!
Christmas was canceled? All elves have the flu?
The kindhearted friends knew just what to do!

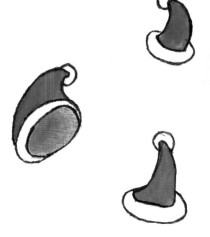

Santa *must* come first.
No more time for play.
There were only six hours
to save Christmas Day!

Vissy sorted the mail.
No letter could be missed.

Penni settled in
to complete Santa's list.

Flash and Zing,
with hammers and saws,
built train tracks for trains
and doll houses for dolls.

Tess gathered
wrapping paper,
tissue, and bows.

Rain wrapped and tied,
that takes time (all moms know)!

Oh dear!
Transportation was missing!
No reindeer? No sleigh?
One more Spriitelee was needed
to save Christmas Day!

The only one left to help with this job
was the Spriitelee-in-training, this fellow named Bob.
"I'm not ready for this!
I still want to have fun!
Besides, I'm too small
to help anyone."

"Come look for me!" Bob called,
playing hide and seek.
Penni, Flash, and Vissy answered,
"We have no time to peek!"

"Everyone is busy
but I have nothing to do,"
Bob muttered out loud
looking cross, sounding blue.

Running and stumbling while trying to explore,
Bob saw...Santa? But he couldn't be sure.
Yes, his suit *was* red, and his beard *was* white,
but that man by the fire *was no* jolly sight!

Bob was startled to see Santa cry.
He decided right then
it was important to try.
Outside he declared
with a big, mighty shout,
"Santa, I'm ready!
I *will* help you out!"

Bob didn't panic. Bob kept his cool,
climbing onto the seat of a rickety stool.
Lining up reindeer in two perfect rows,
tightening harnesses, tying on bows.

With the reindeer all set,
the biggest job still ahead,
a small boy had to pull
the huge sleigh from its shed!

Bob flexed his muscle.
(Not much of a lump!)
The sleigh wouldn't budge.
Poor Bob was stumped.

He thought of a plan and dug deep lines in the snow.
Then he pushed super hard and let the sleigh go.
Slipping and sliding it slid down the hill,
right to Santa's front door, finally ready to fill!

"I helped Santa!" Bob cheered with surprise and delight,
unaware of great magic stirring that night...

As the moon rose to shine,
Santa saw all was fine.
"A Christmas miracle
in the Saint Nick of time!"

His smile, it glowed.
The room burst with joy.
"Ho, Ho, Ho! Little Spriitelees,
please choose a toy!"

Zing floated a boat,

Tess flew a kite,

Rain kicked a soccer ball,

Flash rode a bike.

Penni played music and

Vissy tied new shoes.

Then they all turned to Bob to see what he would choose.

Bob stepped up to Santa,

no gift in his hand.

"Excuse me Sir, please understand.

The gift that I got isn't one you can wrap.

It's this smile on my face and look at my back!

You want to thank us, but I want to thank you!

See my new sparkpack? Helping *you*, helped *me* too."

"Goodbye Santa! We must leave the North Pole.
Tomorrow is Christmas in Kindness Grove Knoll!"

Dear Grown-ups,
Its as Easy as 1-2-3!

1. Show your child the Sparktificate on the other side

2. Encourage your child to complete 3 kind acts

3. Tear out and personalize the Sparktificate

Children can frame it and proudly show it others.
If friends get inspired, hooray!
After all, the Spriitelee Motto Is: Every **i** Makes a Difference!

Check out www.spriitelee.com to see what other children have done.
Let us know your incredible contributions to brightening our world.

Honorary
Spriitelee Sparktificate

As of _____

I, _____ **am an Honorary Spriitelee**

I brighten the world with my kindness!

I want my world to feel
like Kindness Grove Knoll.

I promise to keep both i's open
for ways that I can help every day.

I know that small sparks of kindness
can add up to a HUGE light.

Every i makes a difference!

Way to go!

Yes!

Super!

We're proud of you!

Yea!

Kindness sparks kindness!

Great job!

The Spriitelees™
Every i makes a difference
Brightening the World with Kindness